I0577449

To Evan & Noah,

May you always hear God's
heartbeat in your life.

God Bless

AFRICAN HEARTBEAT

BY BARB CHRISTING

ILLUSTRATIONS BY PHILLIP CISNEROS

Copyright © 2011 Barb Christing and Phillip Cisneros
Editorial director: Milana McLead
Project editor: Laurie Delgatto
Contributing editors: Jane Sutton-Redner, Ryan Smith
Design and copyediting: Creative Solutions, World Vision U.S.
Sales and distribution manager: Jojo Palmer

African Heartbeat may not be reproduced without the written permission of the author and illustrator.
Contact World Vision, Inc., at World Vision Resources, Mail Stop 321, P.O. Box 9716, Federal Way, WA 98063-9716;
wvresources@worldvision.org.

Production date: 03-02-2011
Plant and location: Everbest Printing Company in Guangdong, China
Job - batch number: 86280

ISBN 978-0-9819235-1-2

Printed in China

To Katie.

You are my joy and God's delight.

—B.C.

For Gabrielle, Ava, and Lex—

thanks for always believing in me.

—P.C.

Meet Katie.

She's 6 and she wants to go to Africa.

The only problem is, it takes a **_gazillion_** steps to get there.

But Katie knows the **bigger** your heart gets, the _smaller_ the world gets.

She learned this from a song her mother taught her:

"Love turns strangers into friends,
It crosses many river bends.
In time love melts the miles away,
And in your heart your friends
will stay."

BOOM-BITTY-BOOM-BITTY-BOOM.

Can you hear that?

I think Katie's heart is
growing. So Africa must
be getting closer.

Katie's dream to go to Africa started the day she met **Neema**.
When she saw Neema's face, she knew she had found her new big sister.

"I pick her, Mama."

She was *sooooooo* excited, her heart began to beat like a drum.

BOOM-BITTY-BOOM
AND A RAT-A-TAT-TAT.

SPONSORSHIP
SUNDAY

Neema and her friend giggled with excitement.

"Oh, Zawadi, I have a sponsor.
A family in America has chosen *me*."

Many of the children in their village were getting sponsors.
Their hearts fluttered with the hope that their lives
would soon be better.

4

"Dear Neema, You are my best . . ."

"Mom, how do you spell *friend*?"

Katie had so much she wanted to ask Neema.
Neema was 9 years old, so Katie knew
she must be very, very smart and very, very big.
But she wondered if Neema
could run as fast as
the wind.

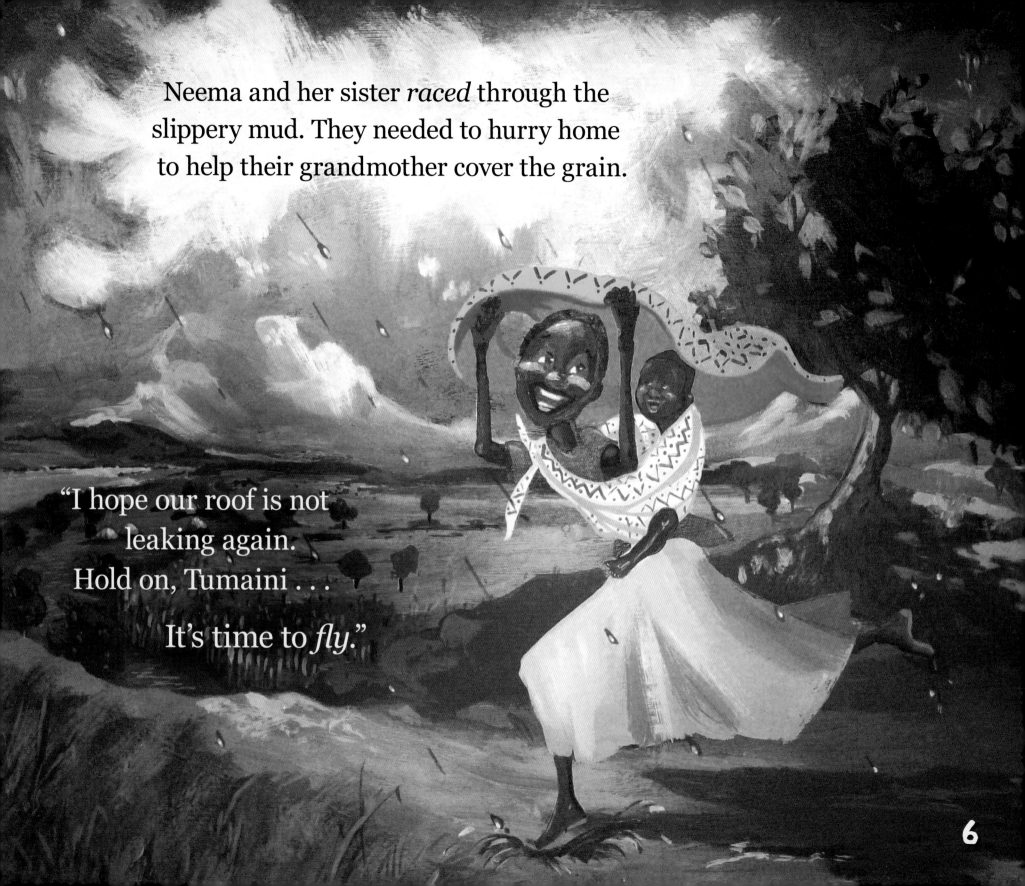

Neema and her sister *raced* through the slippery mud. They needed to hurry home to help their grandmother cover the grain.

"I hope our roof is not leaking again. Hold on, Tumaini . . .

It's time to *fly*."

6

"Mom, why did Neema's mom and dad die?"

"In Africa, many people have a terrible sickness called AIDS," answered Katie's mom. "And they have no money to buy the medicine that can help them feel better."

Katie *jumped* off her chair
and disappeared into her room.

8

When she returned, she was carrying
her piggy bank.

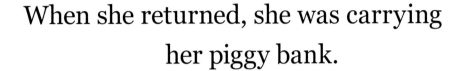

"Then we **must** send them the money,"
insisted Katie, "so that no more
mommies and daddies die."

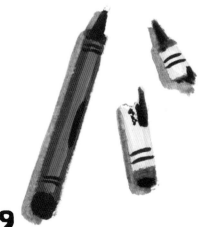

Katie's mom gave her a kiss. "Yes, Katie, we must send them the money . . . and ask God to make everyone as sweet as you."

BOOM-BITTY-BOOM AND A RAT-A-TAT-TAT AND A BINGITY-BANGITY-BONG.

Katie's heart **danced** in her chest. Helping others felt great.

"Grandmother, will I see Mama and Papa again?"

"Yes, Neema. You will see them in heaven someday.
Now run and get some water, child. It is time to prepare
the evening meal."

12

"Look, Mom!

I found the perfect apple. I wish Neema
was here. We could bake a pie together."

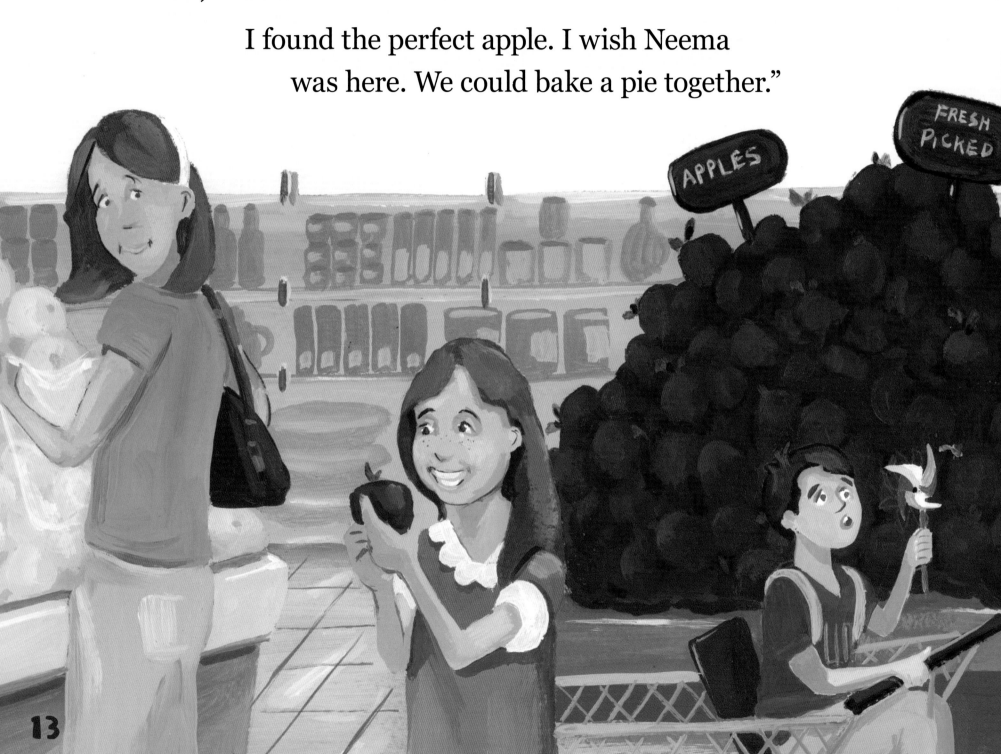

"Look how big the corn is this
    year, Grandmother!

   I wish Katie was here.
      We would have a feast."

14

"Hey, Dad, if I throw this ball far enough, will it get to Neema?"

Katie's dad laughed. "No, Katie. Africa is a world away."

"But Dad . . .

BOOM-BITTY-BOOM

. . . Africa is getting closer . . .

RAT-A-TAT-TAT

. . . every day!"

BINGITY-BANGITY-BONG.

Kicking the ball high into the sky, Katie yelled with glee, "Here you go, Neema. Catch!"

Neema's heart skipped a beat when she saw the beautiful ball.

"Oh, Grandmother, Katie has sent me a present.
A present for *me*!
May I show it to my friends?"

"Yes, yes, go. But be back
in time to tend the garden."

17

"*Throw it here, Neema!*"

"*No, no. Give it to me!*"

Neema and her friends laughed and played in the sun. If you listen closely, you can hear their hearts singing.

BOOM-BITTY-BOOM. BITTY-BOOM.

"*Thank you, Katie,*" Neema shouted with joy as she tossed the ball high into the air.

18

Katie loved summer. It was sunny and hot and so much fun. As she splashed in her pool, she wondered what Neema was doing.

"Cannonball!"

"The new school is almost finished, Neema . . .

"Just think, soon we will have books and pencils and a real teacher."

21

Neema bubbled with excitement. "We must study hard, Zawadi. Then maybe someday we can go to college."

Her heart *raced* all the way home.

BOOM-BITTY-BOOM
AND A
RAT-A-TAT-TAT
AND A
BINGITY-BANGITY-BONG.

"*Dear Katie, You are such a good friend. When will you visit me? I want to show you the new baby pigs. The men of the village are so proud of them. We danced and sang all night when they were born.*"

BOOM-BITTY-BOOM. BITTY-BOOM.

Katie thought her heart would jump
right out of her chest.

"Mom, can I go? Can I visit Neema? P-L-E-A-S-E!

Every day my heart is getting bigger and bigger.
And every day Africa is getting closer and
closer. Please let me go.

P-L-E-A-S-E!"

"I'm going to Africa. I'm going to meet my sister Neema!"

"You have a sister in *Africa*?"

"Yup! I bet you have a sister there too. All you have to do is look in your heart to find her."

25

"My sponsor is coming!"

Neema's heart beat with a
BOOM-BITTY-BOOM
AND A RAT-A-TAT-TAT.

"Oh, Zawadi, I must make her a gift."

26

In a heartbeat, Katie's world and Neema's world met.

"I made this for you, Neema. It's a friendship bracelet. Do you like it?"

The bracelet was beautiful. Neema knew she would treasure it forever. She still could not believe that this family from so far away had done so much for her and her village.

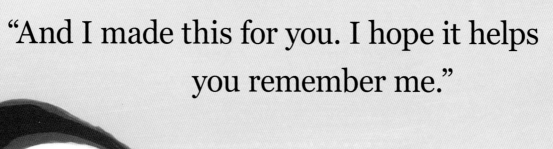

"And I made this for you. I hope it helps you remember me."

Katie giggled. How could she forget Neema? Their friendship was just beginning.

28

Katie and Neema were from different worlds, but they shared the same heart.

"Dear God, thank you for Neema. Keep her safe, and let me see her again someday soon."

BOOM-BITTY-BOOM.

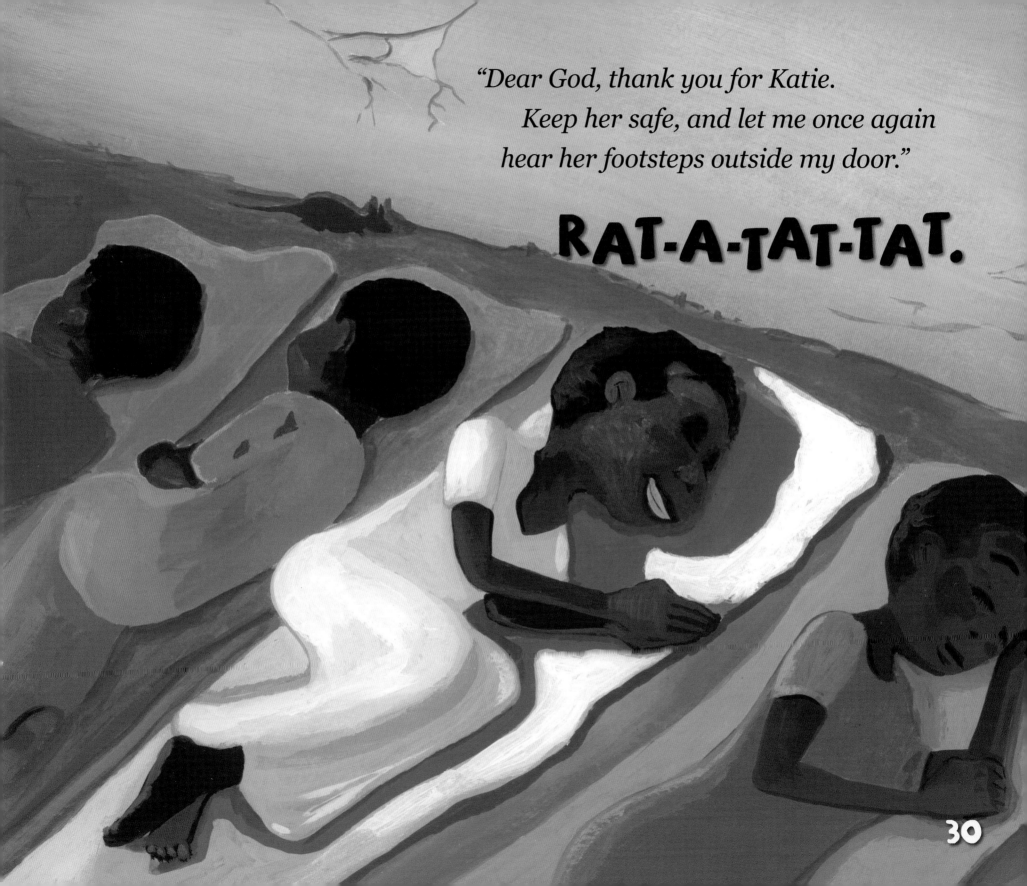

"*Dear God, thank you for Katie.
Keep her safe, and let me once again
hear her footsteps outside my door.*"

RAT-A-TAT-TAT.

Katie knew she would see Neema again someday.
After all, Africa is right around the corner.

"Our hearts are growing one beat at a time.
I can see your world and you can see mine.
Deep down we are family, we know it is true . . .

BOOM-BITTY-BOOM-BITTY-BOOM-BITTY-BOO."

A Guide for Parents and Educators

African Heartbeat is a story about transformation. It highlights the positive spiritual and physical changes that occur on both sides of the ocean during the child sponsorship process. The information contained here is designed to help you understand Neema's world before and after sponsorship. We hope you will use this information to help young readers see the whole story. As you read *African Heartbeat*, encourage the children to take a close look at the illustrations. Ask them how the life of a child in America is different from that of a child in Africa. Encourage them to look for changes in Neema's village as the story progresses (see "How Sponsorship Changes the Landscape"). Together, you and your young readers will discover that while children's circumstances may be different, all children dream of a life of hope and meaning.

Neema's World

African Heartbeat takes place in a small country called Malawi. Nearly 15 million people live in an area the size of Pennsylvania. Malawi is a beautiful country with rolling hills and high plateaus. But it is also a country with much poverty and suffering.

One in eight Malawians is living with HIV or AIDS. Nearly 68,000 of those infected die each year. As a result, more than half a million children in Malawi have lost one or both parents to this deadly disease. The lucky ones, like Neema, are taken in by relatives. The less fortunate are left to fend for themselves in what are known as child-headed households. In these situations, children are raising children in an environment of intense poverty.

In Malawi, children help in every aspect of life. Older children take care of their younger siblings, help prepare meals, work in the fields, and collect water. Young children sweep and help gather sticks for firewood. When time allows, they invent games using sticks, rusty tire rims, and balls made from tightly wound plastic bags.

Ninety percent of the people of Malawi live in rural villages. Their huts are made of mud walls, thatched roofs, and dirt floors. They often have to walk several miles to get water from creeks or ponds for cooking, washing, and bathing. This water is usually full of deadly bacteria and parasites. Diarrhea, caused by bacteria-infested water, is among the top three killers of children under the age of 5.

There are two seasons in Malawi: the rainy season and the dry season. The rainy season begins in October and ends in March. These months are hot and exceptionally wet. Dirt roads and paths become mud bowls, and are often impassable. Crops are planted at the beginning of the rainy season and then guarded against marauding animals like baboons and elephants.

Corn is the main crop in Malawi, and cornfields stretch as far as the eye can see. Most meals consist of corn, with a sprinkling of other vegetables such as pumpkin leaves (see pages 11 and 12). To make the leaves edible, the hairy skin is carefully peeled off before the leaves are boiled. Occasionally, a meal also includes fish or meat.

The dry season lasts from April through September. It can get surprisingly cold during these months, even though the sun turns the country into a dry and barren landscape. These are the "hungry months" as food supplies and natural water sources dry up. Education is valued in Malawi, but there are few resources to help in the teaching process. Many rural classrooms consist of nothing more than a circle of rocks placed under the shade of a big tree (see page 4).

Africa is a large continent consisting of 53 countries. Since many people in Africa speak Swahili as a first or second language, all the African characters in *African Heartbeat* were given Swahili names. Each name has significant meaning.

Neema means "*grace*."

Tumaini means "*hope*."

Zawadi means "*gift*."

How Sponsorship Changes the Landscape

Through child sponsorship, World Vision is working to help Malawians improve their present and future circumstances. Take a close look at the illustrations listed below to see how sponsorship makes a difference.

Before Sponsorship		After Sponsorship	
Page	Look for	Page	Look for
4	Dirty, tattered clothes	21	Clean, new clothes
4	Girls sitting on rocks in a typical outdoor classroom	18	New school construction
--	-----	14	Healthy crops as a result of improved farming techniques
11–12	Unsafe watering hole	21	New well with clean, safe water
--	-----	17	Letters and gifts from sponsors that bring joy
--	-----	22	Hope for a brighter future

About World Vision

World Vision is a Christian humanitarian organization dedicated to working with children, families, and their communities worldwide to reach their full potential by tackling the causes of poverty and injustice. Motivated by our faith in Jesus Christ, World Vision serves alongside the poor and oppressed as a demonstration of God's unconditional love for all people.

We envision a world where each child experiences "fullness of life" as described in John 10:10. We know this can be achieved only by addressing the problems of poverty and injustice in a holistic way. World Vision is unique in bringing 60 years of experience in three key areas to help children and families thrive: emergency relief, long-term development, and advocacy. We bring our skills across many areas of expertise to each community where we work, enabling us to support children's physical, social, emotional, and spiritual well-being.

Visit us at **www.worldvision.org**.

About World Vision Resources

Ending global poverty and injustice begins with education: understanding the magnitude and causes of poverty, its impact on human dignity, and our connection to those in need around the world.

World Vision Resources is the publishing ministry of World Vision. World Vision Resources educates Christians about global poverty, inspires them to respond, and equips them with innovative resources to make a difference in the world.

For more information, contact:
World Vision Resources
Mail Stop 321
P.O. Box 9716
Federal Way, WA 98063-9716
Fax: 253-815-3340
wvresources@worldvision.org
www.worldvisionresources.com